ERIK BROOKS

STERLING CHILDREN'S BOOKS
New York

On his last day,

Alligator said goodbye . . .

Later, Gator!

See you soon, Baboon.

. . . to EVERYONE!

Later, Gator!

Hang loose, Mongoose.

Later, Gator!

I—I gotta go, Buffalo . . .

And then he had to go.

Later, Gator!

His things were packed for a long trip . . .

MOVE ALL
MOVE ALL

. . . to a new place . . .

. . . where Gator was all alone.

He missed his old friends.

A LOT!

Dear Crocodile, Baboon, Mongoose, and Buffalo...

He mailed the letters.

And his friends missed him back!

Which made Gator smile . . .

and gave him an idea.

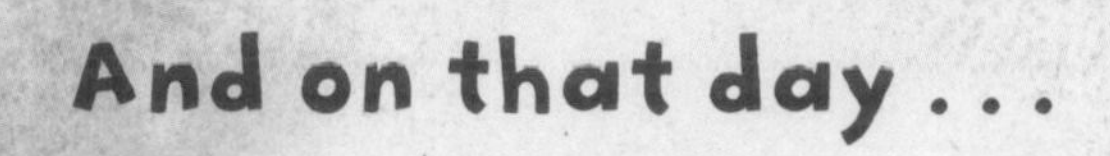

And on that day . . .

Gator said, "Hello!" . . .

Howdy do, Kangaroo!

Hi, guy!

Hey there, Panda Bear!

. . . to EVERYONE!

Hi, guy!

Hello, Gecko!

Hi, guy!

Afternoon, Raccoon!

Hi, guy!

And it was easier than he thought.

Dear Mongoose,

My new friend Kangaroo gets HUGE air on her sled. Miss you, but

For the Casey family—from Winthrop to Tirana to Antananarivo and beyond! —E.B.

STERLING CHILDREN'S BOOKS
New York

An Imprint of Sterling Publishing
1166 Avenue of the Americas
New York, NY 10036

ISBN 978-1-4549-1816-5

Distributed in Canada by Sterling Publishing, Co., Inc.
c/o Canadian Manda Group, 664 Annette Street
Toronto, Ontario, Canada M6S 2C8
Distributed in the United Kingdom by GMC Distribution Services
Castle Place, 166 High Street, Lewes, East Sussex, England BN7 1XU
Distributed in Australia by Capricorn Link (Australia) Pty. Ltd.
P.O. Box 704, Windsor, NSW 2756, Australia

For information about custom editions, special sales, and premium and corporate purchases, please contact Sterling Special Sales at 800-805-5489 or specialsales@sterlingpublishing.com.

Manufactured in China
Lot #:
2 4 6 8 10 9 7 5 3 1
05/16

www.sterlingpublishing.com

The artwork for this book was created using watercolor and acrylic ink.
Design by Merideth Harte

KNOCK KNOCK JOKES